MEET ALL THESE FRIENDS IN BUZZ BOOKS:

Thomas the Tank Engine
The Animals of Farthing Wood
Fireman Sam
Looney Tunes
Bugs Bunny
Flintstones
Joshua Jones
Rupert

First published in Great Britain 1993
by Buzz Books
an imprint of Reed International Books Limited
Michelin House, 81 Fulham Road, London SW3 6RB
and Auckland, Melbourne, Singapore and Toronto

Rupert Characters™ & © 1993 Express Newspapers plc.
Licensed by Nelvana Marketing Inc.,
U.K. representatives: Abbey Home Entertainment Licensing
Text © copyright 1993 Methuen Children's Books
Illustrations © copyright 1993 Methuen Children's Books

ISBN 1 85591 2856

Printed in Italy by Olivotto

RUPERT
and the
VANISHING SCARECROW

Story by Norman Redfern
Illustrations by SPJ Design

Dr Chimp walked into the classroom and opened the register.

"We have a new pupil starting this term," he told the class. "Kevin's family has only just moved to Nutwood, and he hasn't made any friends yet."

Doctor Chimp looked round the classroom.

6

"Would one of you like to show him around the school?" he asked.

At once, the pupils all put up their hands.

"Good," said the teacher. "I can see that Kevin is going to be well looked after. Rupert, I asked Kevin to wait in my office. Please bring him to meet the class."

Rupert was pleased. He walked happily out of the classroom and down the corridor to the teacher's office. The door was open.

"Kevin!" he called from outside the office.

There was no reply, so Rupert walked in and looked all around the room. The office was empty!

Rupert had an idea. He went back down the corridor and into the cloakroom.

"Kevin! Are you in here?" he asked.

There was no answer, but through the window Rupert saw a boy running out of the school gates.

Doctor Chimp was standing outside the
cloakroom. He looked cross.

"I asked you to fetch Kevin from my office,
Rupert," he began.

"He isn't there, Doctor Chimp!" cried Rupert.
"Your office is empty, and I just saw a boy run
out of the gates!"

Back in the classroom, the teacher told the class that Kevin had run away.

"He's new to Nutwood," said Bill Badger. "He might get lost."

"He must be found," said Doctor Chimp. "I will inform Constable Growler at once."

Rupert was worried.

"It's very cold outside. Shouldn't we look for Kevin, too?" he asked.

Doctor Chimp agreed. "This wintry spell is no weather for runaways," he said. "We will send out a search party!"

Outside, Constable Growler took charge of the hunt. He split the class into small groups. Some were sent to search the village, while others followed the road to Popton.

"Rupert, you take Bingo and Podgy," said the policeman. "See if there's any sign of Kevin down on the fields!"

Wrapped up warm in their winter coats, Rupert, Bingo and Podgy set off through the woods. When they reached the other side of the trees, the three friends looked down at the wide green fields.

"Look!" cried Bingo. "Over there!"

"That's not Kevin," laughed Podgy. "That's just a scarecrow!"

"Yes," said Rupert, "but why is it out today? It's far too early to grow corn!"

For a moment, they stared at the scarecrow. Suddenly, Podgy jumped. Something cold and wet had landed on his nose.

"Oh, no!" he shouted. "It's snowing!"

All around them, snowflakes began to swirl in the breeze.

"Kevin isn't here," said Rupert, "and we need somewhere to shelter."

The snow was falling faster and faster, covering the field like a carpet.

"There's a little hut over there," said Bingo, pointing across the field.

The three friends ran to the hut. The door was unlocked, and inside was warm and dry.

16

While the snow fell outside the hut, Rupert, Bingo and Podgy chatted happily inside.

"I wonder if anyone has found Kevin yet," said Bingo.

"I expect so," replied Podgy. "He wouldn't go very far on a day like today!"

After a while, Rupert peered out of the door.

"It's stopped snowing," he said. "Let's go back to Nutwood before it starts again."

He led the way out of the hut and started to crunch through the crisp white snow which covered the field. Then he stopped, puzzled.

"The scarecrow's vanished!" he said, racing across the field to the place where it had been.

"There's no sign of it. But look!" Rupert
exclaimed. "There's a set of footprints in
the snow!"

Bingo pointed out to the others that
scarecrows cannot walk.

"But this one did!" said Podgy. "I bet that
if we followed the footprints, we would find
the scarecrow."

Podgy and Bingo turned away, ready to track down the scarecrow, but Rupert stayed where he was. Something was puzzling him.

"These footprints don't lead away from the spot where the scarecrow was," he told his friends. "They lead right up to the spot — and then stop!"

Podgy tried his foot in the footprint. "You're right," he told Rupert. "That means that someone walked up to the scarecrow, and then simply vanished with it!"

"A scarecrow thief!" said Bingo. "With a friend in a helicopter to make his escape!"

"That's it!" cried Podgy. "Come on! Let's find Constable Growler and tell him!"

Bingo and Podgy set off again eagerly, but Rupert was still thinking.

"I'll catch you up," he called to his friends.

He was sure that no-one would try to fly a helicopter in such bad weather. Who would steal a scarecrow anyway? And why was the scarecrow out so early in the year? The mystery was just beginning, thought Rupert.

He decided to follow the footprints back to where they started.

Rupert tracked the stranger's path across the field. At the edge of the woods, he stopped, surprised. There was another shed, like the one he and his friends had used to keep dry, and the footprints started from its door.

24

Rupert was sure that the answer to the mystery was inside the hut. Slowly, he opened the door. When he saw what was inside the shed, he nearly jumped out of his boots.

There was the scarecrow!

"Hello!" it said. "Who are you?"

"I'm Rupert," said the little bear. "You're Kevin, aren't you? What are you doing here?"

"I was sent to a new school today," said the little boy. "They all knew each other and I didn't know anybody, so I ran away and came to hide in this shed. These old clothes were lying here and — "

26

"You pretended to be a scarecrow!" cried Rupert. "Wait till I tell everyone how you tricked us with your disguise!"

Kevin grinned. He was proud of his plan.

"In fact, I've got a better idea," said Rupert. "Come back to school with me and tell them yourself. They all want to meet you."

"Really?" asked Kevin.

"Really," said Rupert, and he led the way out of the hut into the crisp winter air.

"This way," said Rupert. "By the way, how did you get back here? The footprints all lead away from the hut."

Without a word, Kevin began to walk across the field, backwards.

With each step he left a neat footprint facing
the wrong way.

"I didn't think anyone would find me if I left
a trail leading *away* from the hut," said Kevin.
"But I'm glad you did!"